Cataloging-in-Publication Data (by Cassidy Cataloging)

Otoshi, Kathryn
Two / by Kathryn Otoshi -- 1st ed. -- Novato, CA: KO Kids Books, c2014.
        p. ; cm.
        ISBN: 978-09723946-6-6
        Summary: Two's best friend is One...until Three jumps in between them.
        A powerful story of friendship, loss, letting go, and self-discovery.

        1. Friendship--Juvenile fiction. 2. Separation (Psychology) --Juvenile fiction.
        3. Grief--Juvenile fiction. 4. Self-actualization (Psychology) --Juvenile fiction.
        5. Counting--Juvenile fiction. 6. Number concepts in children--Juvenile fiction.
        7. Courage--Juvenile fiction. 8. [Friendship--Fiction. 9. Separation (Psychology)
        --Fiction. 10. Grief--Fiction. 11. Self-actualization--Fiction. 12. Counting--Fiction.
        13. Numbers--Fiction. 14. Courage--Fiction.] I. Title.

PZ7.O8775 T86 2014

[Fic]--dc23   1409

KO KIDS BOOKS
www.kokidsbooks.com

Distributed by Publishers Group West
www.pgw.com 1-800-788-3123

Printed in China

by Kathryn Otoshi

Two was a playful number.

She was curved on the top, straight on the bottom,
and friendly and warm like the sun.

Her best friend was **One**.
Whenever they'd get the chance — they'd dance!

She'd sing and snap. He'd tappity-tap.

What a pair they made!

At the end of each day, they'd always say,
"One, Two, I'll count on you — 'til the end we'll be best friends."

Until **Three** jumped in 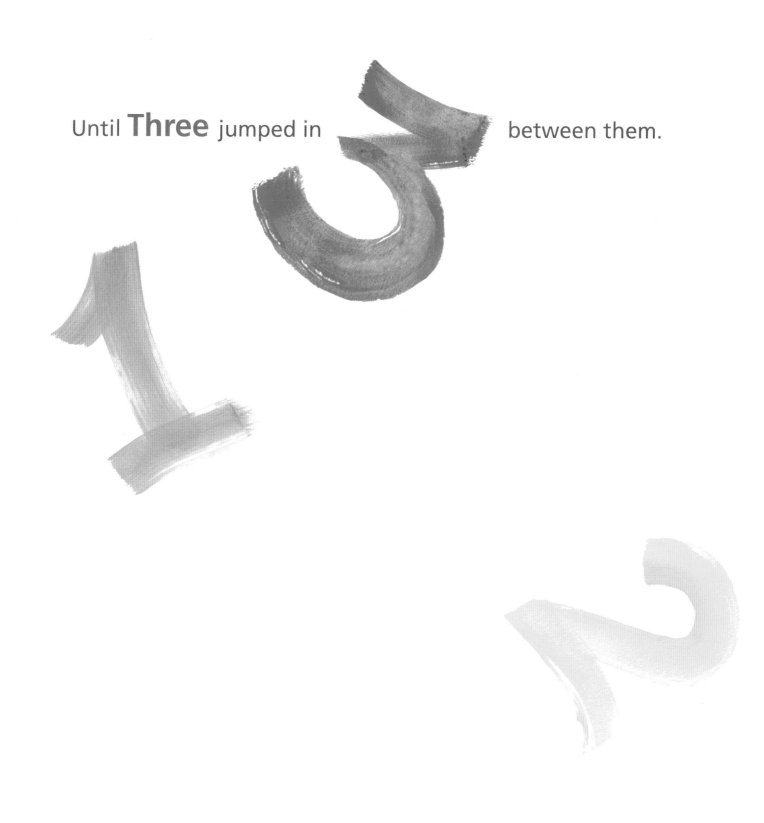 between them.

"You two are like glue!" said **Three**, poking fun.
"Shake things up! Come play with me, One.
Odds are better than the rest,
but One and Three are best!"

1 3 2 5 7 9

Two felt a shift.
She watched One
slowly drift

away

from

her.

Two felt left out.

"Can I play too?" she asked.

"You've had your time to play with One," answered **Three**.

"We're playing *Odds Only* right now."

Two was **blue**. "What did I do? One left without a word. Is it because I'm *even* and they're both *odd*?"

"Let it go," said **Zero**.
"Just ignore them," added **Four**.

But Two couldn't let go.
At every turn, what did she see?
One playing with . . . Three!

"One, Three, *Odds* we'll be!" they'd say.

Two felt . . . a little green.

Her heart felt sick, and she began to **crack!**

The **Evens** rushed over to comfort their friend.

"Such a shame things aren't the same.
Three is silly," said **Four**.

"One can't be best friends with Three.
It's unlucky!" said **Six**.

"One and Three are just plain *odd*.
Let's get *even* with those *Odds!*" exclaimed **Eight**.

Five, **Seven** and **Nine** overheard the chatter.
"What's the matter? There's nothing wrong with being *odd!*"

"*Evens* are great!" stated **Four**, **Six** and **Eight**.

"Sometimes *even GREATER THAN* the *Odds*."

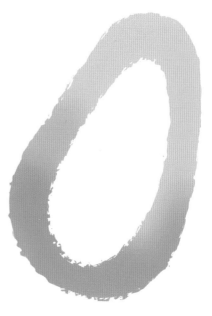

Zero saw the numbers collide.

Why did everyone need to take sides?

"FIVE, SEVEN, NINE!
We're all *odd* and we're just fine!" shouted the **Odds**.

"FOUR, SIX, EIGHT!

Being *even* is first rate!" yelled the **Evens**.

Zero watched this hullabaloo.
She raced over to Two.

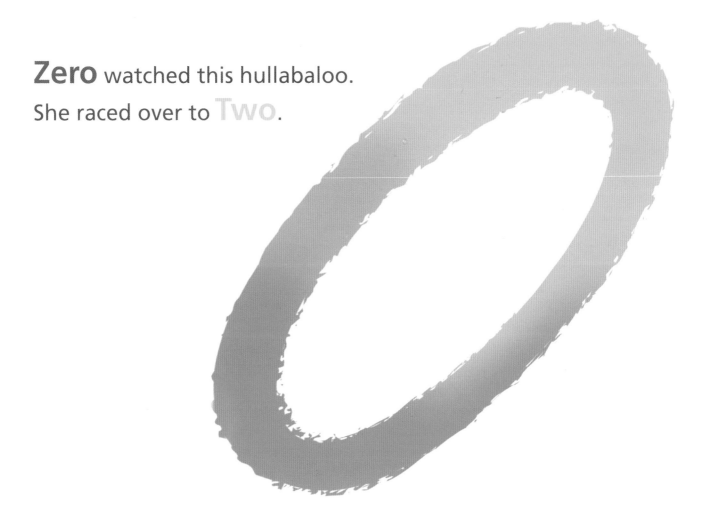

"The numbers are *dividing!*
Now the *Odds* are at *odds* with the *Evens,*
and the *Evens* want to get *even* with the *Odds!*"

Two felt split.

"But what can I do?" she asked.

"Half of me doesn't care about that *odd* pair.
Maybe it's time for me to be done with One?"

"That's the smaller side of you talking!" said **Zero**.
You're *GREATER THAN* that!"

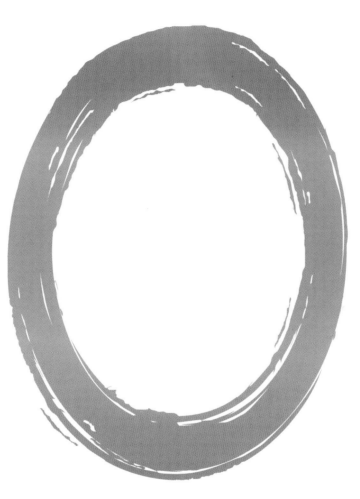

"The *Evens* and *Odds* are in a fight.
What if *you* can make things right?
Can you find it in your heart to see, a new *angle* to this, possibly?"

Two thought . . .

and thought . . .

and then—

"You're right!" she exclaimed, flipping herself around.

"It *is* in me! I can be **LESS THAN** I've been

or **GREATER THAN** I am. The choice is mine."

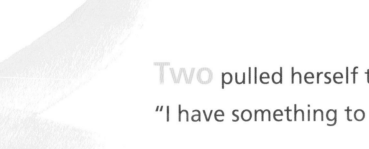

Two pulled herself together and stood up tall.
"I have something to say to you all," she said.

"It's not easy to say, but I've come to see,
it's tricky to dance when there are three. One should
have other friends — and the same goes for me."

Three drooped. "I'm sorry, Two," he said.
"I see now that *playing the odds* wasn't fair to you."

"Well, here's where we can all agree," said Two.

"When the dance turns and shifts, let's groove and flow.

If you're holding too tight — *let go.*

Dance to your own beat. Do your own thing.

Be free to explore what the new day can bring."

"Rock and roll!" said **Seven**.

"Dance and mix," said **Six**.

"Explore!" cheered **Four**.

"*Shake it up!*" they shouted.

Soon all the numbers were dancing together—
movin' and groovin',
shimmyin' and shakin',
and spinning around like tops.

"It's fun to dance with **every**one!" said the numbers.

Two spun faster and faster, 'round and 'round.
She got so dizzy that . . .

OOPS! She bumped into One.

He teetered and toppled and almost fell down . . .

but Two caught him!

"Sorry," said Two.

"Me too," said One.

Both said nothing for a while.
Then One said softly, "Hey, Two. Can I still count on you?"

Two looked at One and said,

"It's the end and guess what . . . ?"

"We're still friends."